TYRANNO QUEST
EARTH ATTACK

Steve Barlow and Steve Skidmore

Illustrated by Jack Lawrence

First published in 2012
by Franklin Watts

Text © Steve Barlow and Steve Skidmore 2012
Illustrations by Jack Lawrence © Franklin Watts 2012
Cover design by Jonathan Hair
The "2Steves" illustrations by Paul Davidson
used by kind permission of Orchard Books

Franklin Watts
338 Euston Road
London NW1 3BH

Franklin Watts Australia
Level 17/207 Kent Street
Sydney, NSW 2000

A CIP catalogue record for this book
is available from the British Library.

ISBN: 978 1 4451 0878 0

1 3 5 7 9 10 8 6 4 2

Printed in Great Britain

How to be a hero

This book is not like others you may have read. You are the hero of this adventure. It is up to you to make decisions that will affect how the adventure unfolds.

Each section of this book is numbered. At the end of most sections, you will have to make a choice. The choice you make will take you to a different section of the book.

Some of your choices will help you to complete the adventure successfully. But choose carefully, some of your decisions could be fatal!

If you fail, then start the adventure again and learn from your mistake.

If you choose correctly you will succeed in your mission.

Don't be a zero, be a hero!

The story so far...

You are a member of a Special Forces military unit. You have been involved in many dangerous missions and have won many medals for your bravery. You are skilled in all forms of combat and weaponry. You have been recruited by Earth Defence to undertake a highly dangerous mission.

Earth Defence is an ultra-secret unit whose job is to defend Earth from attacks by hostile alien forces. The Earth Defence HQ, called Area 61, is based inside a mountain.

You have been given an amazing piece of technology to help you with your quest. It is a Defence Armed-Response Teleportation suit (DART for short). Not only does the suit have an incredible weapons system, but it also allows you to travel to distant planets and different dimensions.

Its inventor is an alien member of Earth Defence, called QTee. He is the technical genius behind all of their weapons and equipment.

↑ **eGun** – main arm-mounted, medium-power weapon, fires energy bolts

↑ **Needle laser** – arm-mounted, light weapon, rapid fire

↑ **Missile launcher** – shoulder-mounted, fires explosive missiles and also QTee's bombs

↑ **NAV system** – a guidance system to help you find your way

↑ **Power unit** – storage cell for crystals that you find

DART suit features

↑ **Speed function** – run twice as fast over a short distance. Also has "super speed" for x4 speed burst.

↑ **Net launcher** – arm-mounted, fires steel web net to catch and snare

Other special features:

Poly-absorption armour

Teleportation unit

Stealth mode — you can sneak past enemies

EARTH DEFENCE
BRIEFING DOCUMENT

IDENTIFICATION OF ENEMY

NAME: TYRANNO — also known as: The Starlord and Emperor Of A Thousand Worlds

HOMEWORLD: The Deathworld

LOCATION: Unknown

AMBITION: To rule all known planets throughout every dimension of time and space

BACKGROUND INFORMATION

Tyranno has placed his followers to rule planets throughout the galaxies and dimensions.

These governors have each been given a Staff of Power that they use to enforce their rule.

Tyranno has ordered that Earth is to be invaded and conquered.

Earth was attacked by Hurrikano, the ruler of Airworld, Vulkana, the ruler of Fireworld and Arktos, the ruler of Iceworld.

You stopped the attacks by travelling to their planets and destroying them. You have also captured the crystals that powered their staffs. QTee has placed them in the DART suit, which means that you now have control over the elements of air, fire and ice.

You will need them, because you know that having defeated Tyranno's followers, the Starlord will now take matters into his own hands...

Go to 1.

1

You are writing up your report of your latest fight against Tyranno's followers, when the emergency alarms ring out across Area 61.

Agent Lee bursts into the room. "We're under attack! We need you in the DART suit now!"

You rush to the OPS room, where Agent Lee is studying the bank of screens on the wall. You stare at them in amazement. "What is that thing?" you ask.

QTee replies, "Scanners indicate that it is some kind of creature made up from elements of metal, rocks and crystals. It seems to have been ripped up from out of the Earth!"

"Do you think this is something to do with Tyranno?" you ask.

QTee nods. "I'm sure it is..."

"Well, wherever that thing has come from, it's trying to smash its way into the base," says Agent Roberts. "We've scrambled the security forces, but normal weapons aren't having any effect on it. It's trying to break through the steel entrance."

You smile. "Then there's no time to lose."
You make your way to the DART suit and step
into it. "Let's get going," you say. "Teleport
me to a position behind the creature. That way
we'll surprise it."

"We don't know what we're dealing with
here," says QTee. "Perhaps we should arm the
suit with some of my special weapons."

**If you want to attack the creature
immediately, go to 15.**

**If you want to arm the suit with special
weapons, go to 36.**

2

"Attack with ice," you order.

Jets of cold water pour from the weapon
system and immediately freeze on contact
with the skeleton droids. Your enemies are
imprisoned in huge blocks of ice. They cannot
move and their weapons are useless.

"Stay cool," you say as you make your way
past the droids and head onwards to your
showdown with Tyranno.

Go to 22.

3

The light disappears and you find yourself drifting in space. Thousands of stars twinkle in the blackness of the void.

"Where am I?" you ask.

"Unknown location," reports the suit.

"Teleport to Earth," you say in desperation.

"Unable to locate Earth," the suit replies. "All systems failing..."

You look into the vastness of the universe knowing that this is the end for you. Soon your air supply will run out...

You have become just another piece of space debris. Begin your quest again by going to 1.

4

You look at the screen. "All right. What do you want?"

Tyranno smiles. "So you are the creature who managed to defeat my followers?"

You nod. "That's me. What about it?"

"You interest me," replies Tyranno. "You seem to be a worthy adversary. You must have special powers. I wish to meet you."

"Where are you?"

"Closer than you think. Look to the skies!"

QTee switches the screens to look outside.

There is a bright flash and a huge rip opens up in the sky. From it emerges a huge, black, skull-shaped artificial planet!

"The Deathworld!" says QTee. "It's torn through the dimensions of space! It must have been heading to Earth while we were dealing with Tyranno's followers."

Tyranno speaks. "So will you meet me? I am told you can teleport. I will send the co-ordinates..."

If you want to agree to Tyranno's request, go to 23.

If you want to ask for time to consider Tyranno's request, go to 33.

If you don't want to meet Tyranno, go to 12.

5

"Let's get on with the mission," you say.

At that moment, Tyranno's face reappears on the screens. "Enough delays. I am sending the teleportation codes."

QTee programs them into the suit, but makes the slight change you wanted. "Good luck," he whispers.

"Teleport," you order. The familiar white light surrounds you. Seconds later it dies down and you find yourself standing in a huge room, containing a moving 3D map of the universe.

You realise that you are in the heart of the Deathworld.

There are several alien beings floating around the room. They seem to be observing the movement of the stars and planets, and haven't noticed you.

"Identify," you ask the suit.

The suit scans the aliens. "The creatures are known as watchers. I have no other data."

To attack the creatures, go to 45.

If you wish to locate Tyranno, go to 34.

6

As you speed towards your showdown with Tyranno, the suit sounds a warning alarm. "Enemy forces ahead. One hundred metres."

"Reduce speed and scan," you say.

The suit drops gently to the floor and reports to you. "Robot serpents. Highly dangerous."

You know time is running out — you have to make a decision.

To switch to stealth mode and attempt to avoid the creatures, go to 13.

To attack the serpents with your eGun, go to 8.

To attack them with fire, go to 48.

7

You realise that metal ammunition will only add to the creature's power, so you attack it with your eGun.

You blast the creature, but it remains standing. It lurches towards you, its enormous hands reaching out for you.

If you wish to fly away, go to 26.

To continue with your attack, go to 49.

8

You shoot the creatures with your eGun.
Streams of energy blasts hit your enemies and
they explode into atoms. The creatures are no
match for your weaponry and they are soon left
in smouldering pieces.

You speed through the passages of
Deathworld until you reach the star chamber
— Tyranno's control centre. You are surprised
that it is not guarded. You are about to sneak
in when, to your further amazement, the doors
open. A voice booms out.

"Enter!"

If you wish to enter, go to 21.
To shoot into the room first, go to 44.

9

"OK, I'll teleport up. Transfer the co-
ordinates." You turn to QTee. "Program them
into the suit." The inventor does so.

Seconds later there is a flash of light and a
roaring sound as you are teleported through
space. Then the light dies away and you find
yourself in a huge chamber. Ahead of you is

Tyranno. He is sitting on a giant throne.

The Starlord's voice booms out. "Welcome! It is interesting to meet the creature that defeated my followers. In fact I have a proposal for you."

If you wish to take the opportunity to attack Tyranno now, go to 38.

To listen to what he has to say, go to 28.

10

You know that time is running out and you have to take the risk.

You take route one, through the minefield. The star mines hover menacingly in the air. As you approach, some of the mines begin to move towards you. They start to vibrate and flash red.

"Detonation imminent!" warns the suit.

To avoid the minefield, and take route two after all, go to 16.

To try to fly straight through the minefield, go to 35.

To shoot at the star mines with your ice weapon, go to 19.

"Get me out of here," you tell the suit. "Super speed!"

The suit responds, but Tyranno holds up his hands and the whole star chamber lights up with streams of toxic energy beams that pour out from his body. They fill the room, bouncing off the walls and hitting you again and again...

The DART suit's circuits spark and melt. You drop to the ground. "Teleport back to Earth," you whisper.

The suit does not respond. Its systems have been destroyed. You lie there, helpless...

Go to 39.

12

"I don't think so," you reply.

"Very well. You had the opportunity to save your pathetic planet. Goodbye!"

Tyranno disappears and the screens now show what is happening in the skies above Area 61. Thousands of spaceships suddenly appear, firing heavy laser weapons, missiles and bombs. Area 61 rocks as the weapons explode on the mountainside.

QTee shakes his head. "We're finished..." he says.

You can only watch helplessly as Tyranno's forces continue their devastating attack. There is no hope for Earth — Tyranno will soon be its master...

Earth is doomed! If you wish to begin your adventure again, go to 1.

13

I don't have time to fight these, you think.
"Stealth mode."

The suit obeys and you head slowly towards the serpents.

At that moment an alarm bleeps out down the corridors of the Deathworld. The serpents begin speaking to each other. You tell the suit to translate what they are saying.

"The invasion of Earth is about to begin. All forces are to make their way to the spaceship launch bays."

You realise that stealth is too slow, you have to get to Tyranno!

"Super speed!"

You come out of stealth mode, revealing yourself to the serpents. They open their mouths and spit deadly missiles at you! The air is filled with explosions and you are buffeted around.

To try to avoid the attack, go to 31.

To attack the serpents with your eGun, go to 8.

To attack the serpents with fire, go to 48.

14

Before you can begin your attack, QTee's voice crackles through your communications link. "Tyranno knows you are on the Deathworld. He knows we've tricked him! He is going to attack Earth..." Then the signal goes dead.

You know you have to act quickly and get to Tyranno.

The droids storm towards you, firing bolts of energy from their weapons.

You easily evade the incoming bolts and return fire with your eGun. You take out a couple of the skeleton droids, but more join in the attack. You have to change tactics!

If you wish to try and evade the droids, go to 31.

If you wish to attack the droids using your power over ice, go to 2.

If you wish to attack the droids with fire, go to 48.

15

"There's no time for that," you tell the inventor. "I'm sure the missiles and eGun will be good enough to take this thing down. If not,

I can always hit it with some fire or ice." You step into the DART suit and it closes around your body.

"Teleport," you order. A bright light envelops you.

Seconds later, the light fades and you find yourself standing behind the creature. It places its giant hand on the steel doors, which dissolve and pass into the creature's body, causing it to grow even bigger! You realise that you must attack immediately.

To attack the creature with missiles, go to 43.

To attack with your eGun, go to 7.

16

"Avoid the minefield, take route two!" you tell the suit.

Soon you are flying through the dark passages and corridors of the Deathworld. Minutes pass and a gnawing fear grows in your stomach that you are taking too long.

"Increase speed," you order.

But before the suit can respond it gives out a warning. "Enemy ahead. Alien zombies!

Primitive, but dangerous."

The nightmare creatures see you and shuffle towards you. They are slow, but some of them have laser guns. They open fire.

"Evasive action!" you cry.

The suit veers to avoid the incoming laser beams.

If you wish to use your eGun, go to 27.

If you wish to attack with fire, go to 48.

17

"If you don't call off your attack," you tell Tyranno, "I will detonate a vortex bomb. It will send you and all your forces into a dimension beyond time and space."

Tyranno laughs. "And now you have told me about it! You fool!"

Before you can detonate the bomb, Tyranno blasts you with a toxic energy bolt. You drop into blackness.

Some time later you wake up. Tyranno is sitting on his crystal skull throne.

"Why am I still alive?" you ask.

The Starlord laughs. "I wanted you to see the death of your planet and know that no one can stand up against my power."

You look outside and watch as Earth burns under Tyranno's deadly attack, knowing that you have failed to save humanity.

Then Tyranno turns back to you. "I will keep you alive — the last surviving human being. It will be a fate worse than death."

You will spend the rest of your days as Tyranno's pet. Go back to 1.

18

"I'll come up and see you," you reply. "But we'll need a few minutes to reprogram my DART suit to enable your teleportation codes to work."

Tyranno ponders before replying. "Very well, you have ten minutes." The screen goes blank.

QTee immediately begins to work on the suit. "You now have the powers of ice, air and fire embedded in the suit. You have your normal weapons systems, but I'm also going to arm the suit with a vortex bomb. This is a weapon that you should only use as a last resort."

If you want to get on with the mission, go to 5.

If you wish to find out more about the vortex bomb, go to 40.

19

You control your ice power to form a freezing cloud of ice crystals. They filter through the minefield, covering the mines before they can explode. The star mines drop to the floor, encased in a thick sheet of ice.

You continue to take out the mines and have soon cleared the way forward.

"All mines destroyed," announces the suit.

Time is still against you. You have to get to Tyranno as quickly as possible. "Super speed," you order.

Go to 6.

20

You step into the DART suit as QTee begins to attach the weapons and program them into the computer.

Alarms ring out across Area 61. "Get a move

on," yells Agent Lee. "That thing is inside the base!"

Suddenly there is a huge explosion. The OPS room shakes with the force of the blast.

"The creature must have got into the power room!" screams Agent Lee. "You've got to do something!"

But before you can react, another huge explosion rips through the room.

"You took too long," you hear Agent Lee shout as the lights go out. You are crushed as the ceiling collapses.

Get a move on back to 1.

21

You decide to enter the room, cautiously.

You step forward into Tyranno's star chamber. A force field crackles around you. Ahead of you is Tyranno. He is sitting on a giant crystal skull throne.

Tyranno's voice fills the room. "So you decided to try to trick me, you foolish creature! Did you not think that I have been following your every move, ever since you arrived on my world?"

"So why didn't you kill me?" you ask.

"I have my reasons," he replies. "But first I have a proposal for you."

If you want to listen to what Tyranno has to say, go to 28.

If you wish to attack him with your eGun, go to 38.

If you wish to use your control over fire to attack Tyranno, go to 47.

The DART suit's NAV system sends you through the corridors of the Deathworld. You know you have to move quickly to try to stop Tyranno issuing the order to invade Earth. However, the suit suddenly reduces power. "Warning! Star mines ahead!"

"Tell me more," you say.

"Star mines react to light and movement. Highly deadly. Avoidance recommended. Plotting alternative course." The timings flash up on your display.

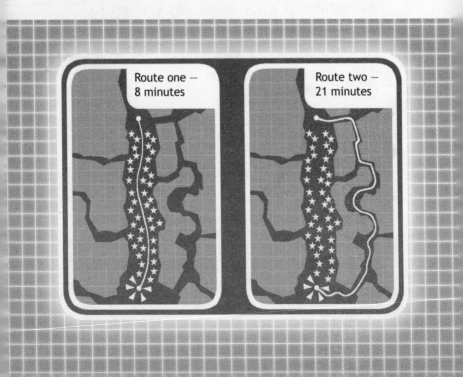

Route one — 8 minutes

Route two — 21 minutes

"Risk of getting through star minefield?" you ask the computer.

It replies, "30 per cent chance of survival."

If you wish to take Route one, through the minefield in the corridor, go to 10.

If you want to take Route two, the longer way round the minefield, go to 16.

23

"OK," you say. "Send over the co-ordinates."

"This is too dangerous," whispers QTee. Agent Roberts and Agent Lee nod in agreement.

You shrug. "It's not every day you get to meet the Emperor Of A Thousand Worlds."

"It will be a trap," says QTee. "You shouldn't go up there."

Tyranno's voice booms out. "Do not listen to these pathetic fools. I will send the co-ordinates for your teleportation up to the Deathworld. I will not give you this chance again."

To teleport to the Deathworld, go to 9.

To ask for more time to consider, go to 33.

If you don't want to meet Tyranno, go to 12.

24

The droids march towards you, firing bolts of energy at you from their weapons.

You easily evade their shots and return fire with your eGun. You hit one of the droids and it explodes into thousands of pieces.

However, more skeleton droids appear. They open fire and the corridor is a mass of explosions as energy blots flash through the air. You realise that you will have to change tactics.

If you wish to try to evade the skeleton droids, go to 31.

If you wish to attack the droids using your power over ice, go to 2.

If you wish to attack the droids with fire, go to 48.

25

"Teleport," you whisper. Nothing happens.

Tyranno moves towards you. "I'm afraid you can't escape. I have blocked all communication links. There is only one way you will leave this place... dead!"

He motions with his hand and you drop to the floor.

If you want to wait to see what Tyranno is going to do, go to 39.

If you wish to detonate the vortex bomb, go to 32.

If you wish to threaten Tyranno with the vortex bomb, go to 17.

26

"Maximum speed," you order. But before the suit can respond, the creature grabs hold of you in its giant hand.

You struggle to free yourself, but the suit has melded onto your enemy's hand. You feel the DART suit melting as the creature absorbs its metal.

Soon the suit has vanished and you cry out in pain. You life force is slowly being sucked from your body as the creature absorbs you, molecule by molecule.

You failed to stop Tyranno's element monster! To begin again, go to 1.

27

You blast the alien zombies with your eGun. Their bodies are ripped apart. You dodge a couple of laser beams, before finishing off the remaining creatures. They are no match for your weaponry. However, you know that time is running out. You have to get to Tyranno before he can order the attack on Earth.

You order the suit to travel at super speed.

As the DART suit speeds you through the corridors of the Deathworld, you see a series of flashing lights ahead of you. You fly towards them.

Go to 37.

28

"Tell me more," you say.

Tyranno laughs. "I propose that you stay here and watch whilst I destroy your planet!"

Before you can react, he holds out his hand. A burst of green energy shoots out and surrounds you. You try to move, but you are trapped. You try to speak, but no sound comes out of your mouth.

"I am surprised that I got you here so easily,"

says Tyranno. "I am amazed that my followers were defeated by you. Still, they were expendable; in fact they were just a diversion. I really wanted the pleasure of destroying your planet myself. And after I have, then I will destroy you, too."

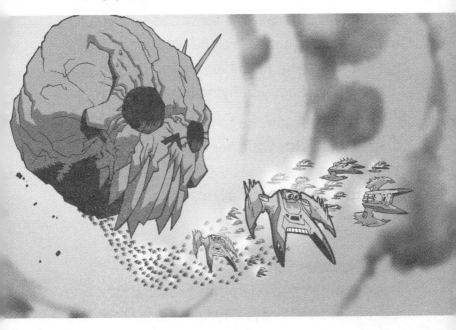

You can do nothing as thousands of spaceships pour out of the Deathworld, heading down to annihilate your beloved planet.

Earth is doomed! To confront Tyranno again, go to 1.

29

"Ice attack," you order. The suit obeys, filling the chamber with snow and ice.

"Super speed," you order. You hurtle towards Tyranno, using the ice storm as a cover.

But before you can reach him, a huge fireball fills the chamber and the snow and ice vanish in a second. Tyranno sees you heading towards him and holds out his hand. A wave of energy hits you and sends you flying backwards.

To try to escape, go to 11.

To attack with your needle laser and missiles, go to 41.

To attack with your eGun, go to 38.

30

Agent Roberts points at a comm-link screen. "We have just picked up this broadcast."

"It's Tyranno," says QTee.

"Where is the signal coming from?" you ask.

"We're not sure," replies Agent Lee. "It seems to be a cross-dimension communication. Our scanners can't pick up anything. He could be anywhere in the universe."

INCOMING CALL_

"What does he want?"

QTee stares at you. "He wants to talk to you!"

If you wish to communicate with Tyranno, the Starlord, go to 4.

If you don't wish to, go to 46.

31

"Avoid attack!" you order the suit.

The suit responds, but your enemy's assault is too ferocious. You are hit time after time, and are sent spinning through the air.

"I can't take any more of this," you shout. "Time to fight back!"

"All weapons systems offline," responds the DART suit. Another blast hits you and you drop to the floor. Pain racks your body, but it doesn't last for long as your enemy moves in and sends you to oblivion.

You have failed. To put a stop to Tyranno, get back to 1.

32

"Arm vortex bomb," you whisper.

"Armed," replies the suit. "Do you wish to launch and detonate?"

You know that this is the only way to defeat Tyranno. You will have to make the supreme sacrifice to save Earth.

Tyranno moves towards you. He smiles. "You have failed, your puny planet is going to be destroyed."

"I don't think so," you reply. "Earth wins! Fire and detonate!"

"No!" cries Tyranno. But he is too late to stop you.

There is a huge blast and a roaring noise as your body is ripped into millions of atoms as the vortex bomb tears open the dimensions of time and space.

Go to 50.

"I need time to think about this," you tell Tyranno. "No offence, but you have declared war on Earth and your followers have tried to kill me, so don't get me wrong, but I don't really trust you."

"I have heard of this Earth humour," replies Tyranno. "I don't understand it. You are a foolish species. Very well, you have two of your Earth minutes to decide." The screen goes blank.

You beckon QTee and the agents to you. "Can you get a fix on the Deathworld?"

QTee shakes his head. "There's a blocking signal on all comm links. You can only teleport when he gives us the co-ordinates and opens the channels."

"But I have to get to the Deathworld if we are going to be able to defeat him."

"It is bound to be a trap," says Agent Lee.

QTee thinks. "I could alter the co-ordinates slightly, so I will get you onto the Deathworld when they open the channel. But it's risky. It might not work. You could be teleported into another dimension and be lost forever."

You groan. "Teleporting isn't much fun at the best of times! Having all your atoms scrambled and then reassembled halfway across the galaxy is bad enough, but the idea that they might not get reassembled at all..."

Agent Roberts looks grimly at you. "It's your call."

The screen flickers back to life. Tyranno appears. "What is your decision?" he asks.

If you don't want to go to the Deathworld, go to 12.

If you wish to use Tyranno's co-ordinates to teleport, go to 9.

If you want QTee to change the co-ordinates, go to 18.

34

"Locate Tyranno," you order the suit.

Seconds later the suit's NAV system displays a diagram of the Deathworld and a route leading to Tyranno.

Leaving the watchers to their task of observing the universe, you move out of the map room and into a long corridor. The walls are made from crystal, layered with scrap and other junk.

You put the suit into stealth mode and cautiously make your way through the corridors of the Deathworld.

Your caution is well founded as the DART suit issues a warning. "Skeleton droid fighters ahead. Highly dangerous!"

If you wish to try to avoid them, go to 42.
If you decide to fight them, go to 14.

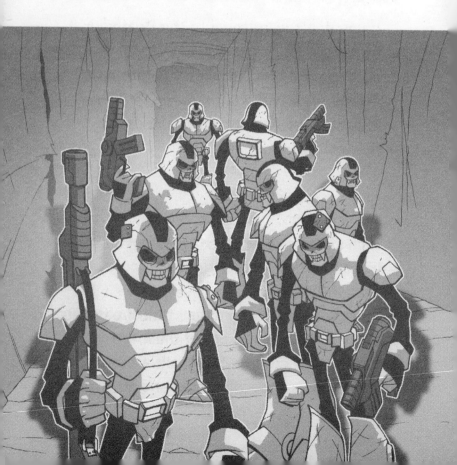

35

"Head through the minefield," you tell the suit.

"14 per cent chance of survival," the computer replies. "Advise caution."

"No time for that!" you say. "Super speed!"

The suit responds. You fly at top speed into the star minefield. In the blink of an eye, the star mines flash red and attach themselves to the DART suit.

You have made a fatal mistake! There is a series of enormous explosions as hundreds of the mines detonate, ripping you apart.

You should have taken more care! If you wish to start your adventure again, go to 1.

36

"What sort of weapons are you thinking of?" you ask QTee.

The inventor smiles. "Some new ones I've been working on."

But before QTee can show you the weapons, Agent Roberts lets out a shout. "The creature's breaking through the main entrance."

"But that's impossible! That steel door is over two metres thick!"

"I'll attach those weapons to the suit and explain what they do," says QTee.

If you want to attack the creature attacking Area 61 immediately, go to 15.

To use the new weapons, go to 20.

37

You find yourself on a huge observation deck, looking out into the vastness of space. The flashes of light are coming from beyond the Deathworld. You look down and you give out a cry of despair. Thousands of Tyranno's spaceships are attacking Earth! The planet is in flames.

The invasion has begun. You watch on, knowing that you have failed. Earth is doomed!

Try to save Earth again. Go back to 1.

38

You point your eGun at Tyranno and shoot him with blasts of energy.

To your amazement, Tyranno's body disintegrates! You smile and think how easy it was to defeat the Starlord.

However, your feeling of victory lasts for

just seconds. There is a roaring noise as the Starlord's molecules swirl around like a tornado. You stand amazed as Tyranno's body re-forms before your eyes.

He laughs. "You cannot kill me! I am the Starlord. My body is made of Star Dust, which I control."

He points at you and a flash of crackling energy shoots from his hand and covers you. Slowly, you feel your body being pulled apart.

You have failed in your quest to defeat Tyranno. Have another shot: go to 1.

39

Tyranno stands over you. "You miserable creature, you have failed! To think you could defeat me. And now I will unleash death on your planet, and you will watch."

You can do nothing as thousands of spaceships pour out of the Deathworld, heading down to annihilate your beloved planet. Tyranno pushes your face against the observation window, and you know that your turn to die will follow shortly.

Your quest is a failure. Go back to 1.

40

"Tell me more about the vortex bomb," you ask the inventor.

QTee looks grim. "It is designed to rip through the fabric of time and space. To put it simply, when the bomb explodes, Tyranno will be blown to atoms and what's left of him will be sent into a dimension outside time and space from which it can never return. Of course, the same thing will happen to anything else within the blast zone."

"How big is the blast zone?" you ask.

QTee shrugs. "I'm not sure, it could be five metres, it could be more. It's a risk we'll have to take."

"You mean it's a risk I'll have to take!"

"Let's hope you can defeat Tyranno without using it," says Agent Lee.

You realise that this mission is going to be your most dangerous and possibly your last.

Go to 5.

You bombard Tyranno with a barrage of missiles and energy bolts, but the Starlord simply absorbs them into his body. He returns to the attack with streams of energy pulses and star missiles. You are sent crashing to the ground.

Before you can recover, Tyranno holds out his hand and a wave of toxic energy surrounds you.

You try to break free, but you are trapped inside a bubble of energy waves. He holds up his hand and raises you from the ground. You

are left hanging in the air.

As Tyranno moves towards you, you glance through the great windows of the chamber and see the Starlord's spaceships pouring out of the Deathworld, heading for Earth.

To detonate the vortex bomb, go to 32.

To threaten Tyranno with the vortex bomb, go to 17.

To try to teleport back to Earth, go to 25.

42

You decide to turn around to avoid the droid skeletons, but as you do an alarm begins to sound in the corridors of the Deathworld.

QTee's voice crackles through your comm link. "Tyranno knows you are on the Deathworld. He knows we've tricked him! He is going to attack Earth…" Then the signal goes dead.

You turn back towards the droids, but by now they have seen you. They hurtle towards you, firing energy bolts.

To attack them with fire, go to 48.

To attack them with your eGun, go to 24.

If you still wish to try to evade the droids, go to 31.

43

"Fire missiles!" you order.

The suit sends a stream of missiles towards your enemy. They burst against the creature's body, but instead of destroying it, the creature seems to absorb the weapons. It grows even bigger as it turns on you.

You realise that the creature is an element monster! It can absorb the Earth's elements. The metal in the missiles is adding to its power! It lumbers towards you, its huge outstretched arms reaching for you.

If you want to fly away, go to 26.
To attack with your eGun, go to 7.

44

"Fire into the room!" you order the suit. It responds and sends a barrage of energy bolts at the opening to Tyranno's control centre.

To your shock, the attack fails — there is a protective force field across the door! The energy bolts bounce back towards you. They shred your armour and knock you down, dead.

Your quest has failed. Go back to 1.

45

I'm taking no chances, you think. "Launch missiles," you order the suit.

You wait a moment, but nothing happens. You repeat your order.

The suit replies. "Unable to respond. There

is a blocking device in this room. All weapons systems are disabled."

At that moment, the watchers turn towards you. Their long tendrils reach through the air and grab hold of you.

"Maximum power!" you order.

The suit replies, "System malfunction."

You try to get away, but it is hopeless. Hundreds of tendrils engulf you and the creatures pull you into the middle of the star map. There is a blinding light as your body is accelerated through space and time.

Go to 3.

46

"I don't think we should talk with him," you reply. "We have nothing to say."

"Shhhh!" QTee shakes his head and points at the screen. "Tyranno's forced open the comm link. He can see us and hear every word we say!"

Tyranno's voice booms out. "Well, Earthling, if you have nothing to say, then I will let my forces do the talking!"

If you now wish to talk to Tyranno, go to 4.
If you still don't want to, go to 12.

Your arm crackles with fire and you launch a scorching hot jet of flame at Tyranno. He is engulfed in a massive fireball.

But your sense of victory is short-lived. The flames die down and Tyranno steps forward through the smoke. He is completely unharmed! "I am the Starlord, you fool. Stars are made of fire, and so am I! Did you really think fire would hurt me? Now it's my turn!"

He points at you and pulses of swirling, fiery gasballs streak towards you. They're like small stars, you think, before they burst around you filling the air with powerful shockwaves. You are sent spinning through the vast chamber. You eventually crash into an observation window and slump to the floor. You stagger to your feet.

"You cannot defeat me!" says the Starlord, laughing loudly.

If you wish to attack with your eGun, go to 38.

If you wish to attack with your ice power, go to 29.

If you wish to try to escape, go to 11.

48

"Attack with fire," you order.

Streams of flame shoot out from the suit's weapons system, engulfing your enemies in a fireball that fills the corridor. You see them melting before your eyes! But your sense of victory lasts just seconds.

In the confined space of the corridor, the fireball explodes and you too are hit by the flames. The intense heat causes the suit to catch fire and instantly begin to melt. "Systems failing," warns the suit. "Systems fail…"

Your skin is exposed to the fire and you feel the heat of the flames. Then thankfully there is no more pain as you slip into blackness.

You are dead. To begin your adventure again, go to 1.

49

You evade the creature's attack and send another deadly stream of energy bolts at it. Again you hit your target! This time the creature succumbs to your attack as it explodes into a million pieces. You shield yourself from the flying debris.

When you look up, there is no trace of the monster. It has become what it once was: part of the Earth.

You head back to the OPS room where QTee, Agent Roberts and Agent Lee are looking very worried.

"What's the problem?" you ask. "I dealt with the creature, didn't I?"

QTee points at the comm-link screen. "We have a bigger problem..."

Go to 30.

The light fades away and the roaring noise stops.

So this is what being dead is like, you think.

"Welcome back!"

You look up. QTee is standing over you, smiling. You are back in Area 61!

Agent Roberts and Agent Lee help you to your feet. You step out of the DART suit.

"What happened?" you ask.

"The suit defaulted to teleport mode," QTee answers. "As soon as the Deathworld comm links were destroyed, we got a fix on you, and here you are!"

"But I was ripped apart by the vortex bomb."

"And put back together when you teleported!" smiles Agent Lee. "You said it yourself, the teleport in your DART suit scrambles your atoms and reassembles them somewhere else. All that happened was that the vortex bomb did the first part for it!"

You shake your head. "What about Tyranno and the Deathworld?"

"Gone into another dimension," replies QTee. "Perhaps into many dimensions, scattered across time and space."

"Do you think he will be back?"

Agent Roberts shrugs. "QTee says not. Me, I'm not so sure. You never know with this job who will pop up next! Anyway, it's time for you to take some rest."

You smile. "Yeah, saving the planet can be a bit tiring!"

Your quest to defeat Tyranno is over, but you know that out there somewhere will be other challenges, and other enemies that you will have to deal with. But whilst you have the DART suit, Earth is safe...for now.

About the 2Steves

"The 2Steves" are
Britain's most popular
writing double act
for young people,
specialising in comedy
and adventure. They

perform regularly in schools and libraries,
and at festivals, taking the power of words
and story to audiences of all ages.

Together they have written many books,
including the *Crime Team* and *iHorror* series.

About the illustrator: Jack Lawrence

Jack Lawrence is a successful freelance
comics illustrator, working on titles such as
A.T.O.M., Cartoon Network, *Doctor Who
Adventures*, 2000 AD, *Gogos Mega Metropolis*
and *Spider-Man Tower of Power*. He also works
as a freelance toy designer.

Jack lives in Maidstone in Kent with
his partner and two cats.

iHorror

Want to read more "You Are The Hero" adventures? Well, try iHorror by the 2Steves.

Check out this sample...

...there is a deafening rumble from beneath the earth, and the ground shakes. The wrestlers look at each other with puzzled expressions. You are immediately on your guard – even two sumo giants can't be heavy enough to cause an earthquake, you think. For a moment there is silence. Then, over the hill behind the stadium, dark clouds gather. Strange lights flash among the seething vapours, and ear-splitting, unearthly cries fill the air.

You look up towards the gathering clouds and realise that something very bad is happening...

‡ *Turn over to the next page.*

1

Suddenly two new wrestlers appear from the hill. They are gigantic: their bodies are bright red, and they have savage expressions with staring eyes, bulbous noses and wide mouths filled with gnashing teeth. One has arms so long that it has to carry them high above its head to avoid tripping over them. The other has tiny arms, but incredibly long legs.

You know that these are not human wrestlers: they are demons. The earthquake that shook the ground must have opened a portal to the underworld, allowing them to escape.

There is complete panic in the stadium as the demon wrestlers leap into the ring. Long-arms hurls the terrified sumo competitors high into the air, and Long-legs stamps around the ring, taunting and jeering at the fleeing audience.

You need to act quickly and decisively, but you have left your weapons in the helicopter. What should you do?

‡ *To head up the hill to get some weapons from the helicopter, go to 64.*
‡ *To use your martial arts skills to attack the demons, go to 30.*
‡ *If you want to think more carefully about what you should do, go to 73.*

Which choice would you make?
Read the rest in

STEVE BARLOW   STEVE SKIDMORE

DEMON
HUNTER

iHorror

Fight your fear. Choose your fate.

978 1 40830 985 8 pb
978 1 40831 476 0 eBook

978 1 40830 986 5 pb
978 1 40831 477 7 eBook

978 1 40830 988 9 pb
978 1 40831 479 1 eBook

978 1 40830 987 2 pb
978 1 40831 478 4 eBook

www.orchardbooks.co.uk